I CAN CHOOSE

By Linda Porter Carlyle   Illustrated by Mark Ford

Edited by Aileen Andres Sox
Designed by Dennis Ferree
Illustrated by Mark Ford
Typeset in 12/14 New Century Schoolbook

ISBN 0-8163-1082-3

92 93 94 95 96 ● 5 4 3 2 1

Dedication

This book is dedicated to Drenon,
who doesn't demand that the lamps be dusted.

Dear Parent,

This book is meant to help you as you teach your child the importance of making good decisions. We need to help our children realize that they do have the power to make decisions about their behavior. And we should emphasize the fact that they will be happier and safer if they make good choices.

So cuddle up on the couch with your child and enjoy this book together. But don't forget that your reading is only part of the learning experience. Listen to your child's responses. Really listen. Take time to talk together. What a powerful thing it is to be a parent!

Linda Porter Carlyle

I Can Choose to Obey

I am going to read you some little stories about boys and girls just like you. Each of the children in these stories has something to decide about obeying. I want you to tell me if the boy or girl obeyed or disobeyed. If they obeyed, put your finger on the Happy Face. If they disobeyed, put your finger on the Stop sign.

Matthew kicked his rubber ball against the side of the garage. The ball rolled back to him, and he kicked it again. He was getting pretty good at kicking balls these days.

The next time the ball rolled back to him, Matthew gave it an extra-hard kick. The ball bounced right past Matthew and out into the street.

"Oh, no," thought Matthew. "I'm not supposed to kick the ball in the front yard, and now it has gone into the street. If I go into the street to get it, I'll be in trouble!"

"Mom," called Matthew, as he ran into the house. "My ball went into the street."

Did Matthew do the right thing when he called his mother for help? Put your finger on the Happy Face or on the Stop sign to show your answer.

Erica pulled her sweat shirt over her head. She had just seen her friend Elizabeth walk into the yard. She wanted to be ready to go outside and play when Eliza-

beth got to the door.

"Erica, did you feed the dog this morning?" asked Mother from the kitchen.

"Yes," answered Erica, poking her arms into the sweat shirt sleeves.

"It's OK," she thought to herself. "I'll give him some extra food tonight. Mama will never know I didn't do it this morning."

Did Erica do the right thing? Put your finger on the Happy Face or on the Stop sign to show your answer.

Lisa and Christine were playing house in the living room at Lisa's house. There was a wonderful smell drifting in from the kitchen. Lisa's mama was baking cookies.

"Girls," called Lisa's mama. "The cookies are out of the oven. Would you each like to have one?"

"Oh, goody!" cried Lisa as she ran to the kitchen. Christine followed behind her.

Lisa took the biggest cookie off the cooling rack. Christine stood and looked at the cookies. They smelled so good!

"Go ahead, Christine. You may have one too." Lisa's mother smiled.

"My mama doesn't like me to eat cookies before supper," said Christine. "May I take one home and eat it later?" she asked.

Did Christine obey her mother? Put your finger on the Happy Face or on the Stop sign to show your answer.

"Now, Joey, I do not want you to get out of bed tonight," said Mama firmly. "After we pray and I tuck you in, I want you to stay in bed."

"OK," answered Joey.

Mama and Joey prayed together. Then Mama tucked the covers in and kissed Joey on the forehead. "You're going to stay in bed now, right?" she asked.

Joey nodded Yes, and Mama turned off the light and left.

Joey lay still for several minutes. Then he heard Buster begin to bark and bark. Why was Buster barking? Joey wanted to know what was going on outside. He pushed the covers back, got up, and went to peek out his window.

Did Joey obey his mother? Put your finger on the Happy Face or on the Stop sign to show your answer.

Jesus wants us to learn to obey. He wants us to be happy. When we obey our parents and teachers, we don't get into trouble for disobeying. We stay safe and happy when we obey. Parents are proud of us when we obey. Jesus is proud of us too.

Chapter 2

I Can Choose to Share

The children in the next few stories each have something to decide about sharing. I want you to tell me if the decision that the boy or girl made was a good decision or a bad one.

Tommy and Steven were playing cars in the front yard. They were making roads for their cars in the dirt under the big maple tree. The trouble started when both boys wanted to drive the only firetruck.

"I want to drive the firetruck now," said Tommy.

"No!" answered Steven. "I'm using it, and it's mine anyway."

"But you've been using it all day," com-

plained Tommy. "Why don't you share?"

"No! I don't want to!" hollered Steven.

Do you think Steven should have shared his truck with Tommy? Put your finger on the Happy Face or on the Stop sign to show your answer.

"Mindy," said Mama as she hung up the phone, "Mrs. McCoy is bringing Kate over to play with you this afternoon."

"Oh, good!" shouted Mindy.

"I want you to share your toys nicely with Kate while she is here," reminded Mama.

"But I don't want her to play with my big baby doll," said Mindy. "Sometimes Kate throws my toys around."

"OK," said Mama. "We'll go right now and put your doll safely away in my bedroom. You have plenty of other toys you can play with."

Put your finger on the Happy Face if you

think Mindy made a good decision about sharing or on the Stop sign if you think she made a bad decision.

Tina and Chelsea were playing house. Tina's mother had given them some wonderful old clothes to play with. They had hats and purses and long dresses and a pair of high-heeled shoes with silver bows.

"I want to be the mother now," said Chelsea, sitting down on the back-porch steps. "It's my turn to wear the high heels."

"OK," said Tina. "We'll take turns."

Did Tina have a kind and sharing spirit? Put your finger on the Happy Face or on the Stop sign to show your answer.

Thomas had just moved next door to José. José was very happy to have another boy the same age living right next door. He invited Thomas to his house to get acquainted.

Raindrops were chasing each other down the windowpane. The two boys sat on the floor in José's bedroom. "You have a great room!" said Thomas, looking around. "You sure have a lot of piggy banks."

"Yep," said José. "I have a piggy-bank collection."

"I want to play with them," said Thomas. "We could play pig farm."

"No," said José quickly. "Some of those banks are breakable. We can play with my other toys. I don't want us to play with my piggy banks."

Do you think José made a good decision about sharing or a bad decision? Put your finger on the Happy Face or on the Stop sign to show your answer.

Remember we don't always have to share everything with everybody. Sometimes we have something special that we just don't want to share. And that's OK. The important thing is to be polite and to have a kind and sharing spirit, not a selfish spirit.

Jesus wants us to learn to share and how to say No nicely. Do you have a kind and sharing spirit?

Chapter 3

I Can Choose How to Act When I'm Disappointed

Something disappointing happens to the children in each of the next few stories. When we are disappointed, we have to decide how we are going to act. If you think the boys and girls acted like Jesus would want them to, put your finger on the Happy Face. If you think the boys and girls made their problems worse, put your finger on the Stop sign. Remember, if we ask Jesus to help us, He will help us make good choices when we are disappointed.

Mary Elizabeth climbed out of the car and took Mama's hand. "I'm too hot!" she said.

"I'm hot too," answered Mama. "But this is the last store we have to go to. When we are finished here, we'll go home."

In the store, Mary Elizabeth followed Mama down the aisles. Suddenly she saw a big bin filled with bright rubber balls. There were balls of every color. "Mama!" shouted Mary Elizabeth, "I want a ball!"

"I'm sorry, Mary Elizabeth," said Mama. "I can't get you a ball today."

Mary Elizabeth's lower lip stuck out. She stamped her feet up and down and began to cry loudly.

Did Mary Elizabeth do the right thing? Put your finger on the Happy Face or on the Stop sign to show your answer.

Terri and Teddy were building a giant tower with their blocks. It was a beautiful tower. It was almost as tall as their heads.

"Be careful!" said Teddy as he watched Terri put on another block. "It's getting wobbly."

Terri stepped back to look at her block. Suddenly the tower collapsed. Terri looked at Teddy. There was a tiny tear in the corner of her eye. "I'm sorry," she said. "I didn't mean to knock it over."

"That's OK," said Teddy, bending down to pick up blocks. "Let's make another one."

Did Terri and Teddy handle their disappointment well? Put your finger on the Happy Face or on the Stop sign to show your answer.

"Willie," called Mama. "Come wash up. It's time to eat."

Willie leaped up the back-porch steps and banged into the kitchen. "What's for supper?" he asked.

"We're having tomato soup and sandwiches," answered Mama.

"Oh, no!" exclaimed Willie. "I hate tomato soup!"

"Willie!" said Mama, "do I want to listen to you complain about supper?"

"I guess not," Willie answered. He grinned. "Is it OK if I only eat a little soup?"

Willie was disappointed that he had to eat tomato soup for supper. Did he handle his disappointment well? Put your finger on the Happy Face or on the Stop sign to show your answer.

Sarah straightened her stuffed rabbit's bow tie and put him carefully on her bed. All of her stuffed animals sat attentively in a row. Sarah was getting ready for Rosa to arrive and play with her.

Mama came to the bedroom door. "Sarah," she said, "Mrs. Gómez just called. Rosa can't come over to play today. She has a sore throat and a fever."

"But I want to play with her!" Sarah exclaimed.

"I know," Mama answered. "But sometimes things don't work out like we planned. It's OK to be disappointed. And it's OK to tell me you are disappointed. But then we will make some new plans for the day."

"I really want to play with Rosa. I'm disappointed she's not coming," Sarah said sadly. "What will I do now, Mama?" she asked.

Sarah was disappointed that she couldn't play with Rosa. Do you know what she decided to do? She painted a picture for Rosa. Do you think Sarah handled her disappointment well? Put your finger on the Happy Face or on the Stop sign to show your answer.

Have you had a disappointment? What did you do when you were disappointed?

14

Chapter 4

I Can Choose to Be Responsible

These stories are about carelessness. Do you know what it means to be careless? It means not taking care of the things that need taking care of. Jesus doesn't want us to be careless. He will help us learn to be responsible when we ask Him to help us.

If you think the children in the story are acting carelessly, put your finger on the Stop sign. If you think the boys and girls are learning to be responsible, put your finger on the Happy Face.

"Here it comes!" shouted Tyler. He ran up to the big red rubber ball and kicked it with all his might. "Go get it! Go get it!" he shouted to Benny.

Benny ran after the ball. He ran across the lawn and followed the big red ball into Mama's flowers. The big red ball and Benny bounced into Mama's tulips.

"Here it comes!" called Benny. He took careful aim and kicked the ball back to his brother. Benny stomped back out of Mama's flower bed.

"Get it! Get it—" shrieked Tyler, as he kicked the ball back to Benny. The big red ball sailed right past Benny and into the tulips . . . again.

Benny chased the ball to the edge of the grass. He stopped and looked at Mama's tulips. Some tulips tilted to the right. Some tulips leaned to the left. Some tulips lay broken on the ground.

"Oh, dear!" said Benny. "Look at Mama's flowers."

Do you think Tyler and Benny were careless about where they kicked their ball? Put your finger on the Happy Face or on the Stop sign to show your answer. Do you think they should go tell Mama what happened to her tulips and that they are sorry?

"Here are the clean towels and wash-cloths," said Mama to Nathan as she put the clothes basket on the couch. "Do you remember how to fold them?"

"I think so," answered Nathan.

"Please go wash your hands first," Mama added as she caught sight of Nathan's grubby fingers.

Nathan washed his hands and returned to the living room. He picked up the top towel and sniffed it. He really liked the smell of fluffy, clean towels.

Nathan lined up the edges of the towel and folded it carefully. He didn't understand why Mama was so particular about folding towels. No one could see them all folded so neatly behind the closet door.

Nathan picked up the second towel and folded it nicely too.

"Are you doing a good job, Nathan?" called Mama from the kitchen.

"Yes, I am," Nathan called back.

Do you think Nathan did his chore of folding towels in a responsible way? Put

your finger on the Happy Face or on the Stop sign to show your answer.

"Nina," said Mama, holding the laundry basket, "where is your new pink sweat shirt?"

Nina looked up from the puzzle she was putting together. "I don't know," she answered.

"Well, I want to wash it," said Mama. "Please go get it."

Nina looked in her bedroom. She looked in her closet. She even looked under her bed. "I can't find it," she called to Mama.

Mama came to the doorway of Nina's room. She did not look happy. "You were wearing it yesterday," she said. "Where did you take it off?"

Nina thought and thought. "I know where it is!" she exclaimed. "I got too hot when I was swinging yesterday. I took it off by the swing set."

Mama sighed. "Go get it," she said.

Do you think Nina was careless with her new sweat shirt? Put your finger on the Happy Face or on the Stop sign to show your answer. It was OK for Nina to take her sweat shirt off when she got too hot. But what should she have done with it when she finished playing?

"Todd," called Mama from the front door. "It's time to come in."

"I'm coming," Todd answered.

Todd and Brian were kneeling under the big oak tree in the yard. They had been busily driving their trucks and cars and Brian's ambulance up and down dusty roads.

"Will you help me pick up my cars?" Todd asked Brian.

"OK," Brian said.

The two boys put the cars and trucks into the cardboard box where Todd kept them. Then Brian stood up and tucked his ambulance under his arm. "I'll see you tomorrow," he said.

Todd stood up and looked around carefully. There were no more cars or trucks underneath the old tree. He picked up his box and went into the house.

Do you think Todd was careless with his toys? Put your finger on the Happy Face or on the Stop sign to show your answer.

Can you think of one time when you were careless? What could you have done to be more responsible?

Chapter 5

I Can Choose to Be Honest

The children in the next few stories each have something to decide about being honest. I want you to tell me if the decision the boy or girl made was a good decision or not.

Eric was swinging in the backyard. If he leaned and stretched his legs as high as he could, he could sometimes touch the tips of the leaves of the big birch tree.

"Eric," called Mama from the kitchen window. "Please come in and get ready to go to the store with me."

"I'm coming," answered Eric. He pumped harder on the swing. He had touched the leaves with his foot nine times. He wanted to do it just once more.

"Eric," called Mama. "Come in the house. We need to leave!"

"I'm coming," said Eric, swinging as high as he could.

Eric said he was coming when Mama called. Was he telling the truth? Put your

finger on the Happy Face or on the Stop sign to show your answer.

Ryan was riding his scooter down the street with his friend Michael. Ryan was very happy. He had wanted a scooter like Michael's for a long time. Now he finally had one. And it was bright red too.

When Ryan and Michael got to Mr. Johnson's house on the corner, Ryan stopped.

"Why are you stopping?" asked Michael.

"My dad says I can't ride farther than

Mr. Johnson's house," Ryan said.

"Well, I can," said Michael. "Let's ride one more block down the street together."

"No," said Ryan. "I'll wait for you here."

Did Ryan obey his dad? Put your finger on the Happy Face or on the Stop sign to show your answer.

Jenny was sitting on the floor in her bedroom. She was surrounded by pieces of her Lincoln Logs set. Playing with the Lincoln Logs was her favorite game. She liked to build houses and make roads to connect them.

"Jenny," called Mother. "It's time to come and help me set the table for supper."

"Oh, no," grumbled Jenny to herself. "I want to finish building this house I'm working on." Jenny sat quietly and pretended that she hadn't heard Mother call.

Was Jenny being honest? Put your finger on the Happy Face or on the Stop sign to show your answer.

"Jeremy," said Daddy with a frown, "the telephone is off the hook. Have you been playing with the phone again?"

Jeremy looked at his feet. He knew he wasn't allowed to play with the phone. And he also knew that it wasn't right to tell lies. "Yes, I have," he said bravely.

Did Jeremy do the right thing when he played with the telephone?

Did Jeremy do the right thing when he told the truth to his daddy? Put your finger on the Happy Face or on the Stop sign to show your answers.

Jesus gave us rules to help make our lives happier. If we don't tell lies, we don't get into trouble for lying. If we obey our parents and teachers, we don't get into trouble for disobeying. Jesus wants us to be happy and honest people. Look for chances to obey the rules that Jesus gave us even when no one is watching.

Chapter 6

I Can Choose to Be Safe

These children each have something to decide about obeying safety rules. After each story, I want you to tell me if the decision the boy or girl made was a good one.

Candi and Yolanda were sitting on the bedroom floor. They were happily coloring pictures.

"I want to cut out this doll I colored," said Candi. "Where are your scissors?"

"I have special scissors," answered Yolanda. She got up and went to her desk to find them. The desk was piled with papers and books and pencils and toys. Yolanda dug around a bit, looking for her scissors. "I can't find them," she sighed.

"Well, get another pair," said Candi. "I want to cut out my picture."

"I'm not supposed to use Mama's scissors," said Yolanda.

"Oh, it's all right," said Candi. "Your mama won't care if we use them and put

them right back."

"OK," said Yolanda, "I'll get them."

Did Yolanda make a good decision when she went to get her mama's scissors? Put your finger on the Happy Face or on the Stop sign to show your answer.

Thomas came in the back door. He sniffed hungrily. Supper was cooking on the stove, and it smelled good! He looked around for Mama, but she wasn't in the kitchen.

"Hi, Thomas!" called Mama's voice. "I'm in the bathroom. I'll be out in a minute."

Thomas sniffed again. He wondered what was cooking. He dropped his big blue-and-red ball and his sweat shirt on the floor and wandered over to the stove. Maybe he would look to see what was in the kettles.

Thomas dragged a chair over to the stove. He climbed up and stood on the chair. He reached over to lift the lid off one of the kettles.

Did Thomas make a good decision when he climbed on the chair to look in the hot kettle? Put your finger on the Happy Face or on the Stop sign to show your answer.

Frederick sat on the steps of his apartment house. The sun shone on him warmly, and Mrs. Brandt's cat curled contentedly in his arms. Frederick smiled as he stroked the cat's soft fur. He always liked holding Mrs. Brandt's cat.

Suddenly Mr. Peter's dog trotted around the corner. Frederick frowned. Mrs. Brandt's cat did not like Mr. Peter's dog.

Mrs. Brandt's cat looked at the dog. She leaped off Frederick's lap. The dog saw the cat and barked happily as he chased her down the sidewalk.

"Stop! Stop!" shouted Frederick, running along after them.

Suddenly Mrs. Brandt's cat dashed into the street. Mr. Peter's dog followed her. Frederick stopped at the curb. He was not allowed to go into the street.

Did Frederick make the right decision when he stopped and did not follow the dog and cat into the street? Put your finger on the Happy Face or on the Stop sign to show your answer.

Jesus gave us grown-ups in our lives to help keep us safe. One of their jobs is to teach us safety rules. Can you tell me two or three safety rules that you have been taught?

Are you going to ask Jesus to help you obey the safety rules that you know? Put your finger on the Happy Face or on the Stop sign to show your answer.

Chapter 7

I Can Choose to Be Kind

The children in these stories each have something to decide about how they treat other people. After each story, I want you to tell me if the decision that the boys or girls made was a kind one. If it was a good decision, put your finger on the Happy Face. If it was a bad decision, put your finger on the Stop sign.

Carmen and Annie sat together on the dusty ground under the big maple tree. The sunlight shone down through the nearly bare branches and made pretty shadow patterns on the ground beside them. Carmen was singing a soft little song. Annie was drawing pictures with a twig in the dirt.

Suddenly Carmen looked up. She saw someone leaning on the fence by the sidewalk, watching them. "Look," whispered Carmen, "there's that new girl. I don't like her."

Annie looked up at the new girl. "Go away!" she shouted. "You can't come in my yard!"

Did Carmen and Annie make a good decision about how to treat the new girl on the block? Put your finger on the Happy Face or on the Stop sign to show your answer.

"I get to feed the fish at school today," Kenny told Mama excitedly. "Hurry up!

Drive faster!"

Mama laughed. "I can't go through a red light," she said. "But I'm hurrying."

Finally Mama pulled the car close to the curb in front of Kenny's school.

Kenny jumped out of the car and raced up the walk to the school door. He banged into his classroom and ran over to the fish tank. Nate was kneeling on the table, looking down into the fish tank. "They were sure hungry!" said Nate. "Just look at them gobble their food."

"Hey!" shouted Kenny. "It's my day to feed the fish!" He shoved Nate off the table. "I hate you!" he said.

Did Kenny make a good decision about how to treat Nate? Put your finger on the Happy Face or on the Stop sign to show your answer.

Adam was feeling very shy. He sat low in the seat and didn't even look out the car window. Mama was starting a new job today. Adam would be spending his day at Mrs. Peel's Day Care. Adam already knew Mrs. Peel. He even liked her. But he didn't want things to change. He wanted Mama to stay home with him.

Mama parked in front of Mrs. Peel's house. Adam climbed slowly out of the car.

"Hi, Adam!" called Mrs. Peel. "Come on over and meet the gang." Mrs. Peel was kneeling on the grass at the side of the yard. There were children crowded around her. She waved at Adam with the little garden shovel in her hand.

"Hi, Adam!"

"Come over here!"

"We're planting tulips!"

"Come on, Adam!" the children called and waved.

Did the children at Mrs. Peel's Day Care make a good decision about how to treat the new boy, Adam? Put your finger on the Happy Face or on the Stop sign to show your answer.

Jesus came to our earth to show us how much He loves each of us. He wants us to remember that everyone we meet is a child of God. Can you ask Jesus to help you treat other people kindly and carefully?

Chapter 8

I Can Choose to Work Well

These children each have a job to do. Their mommies and daddies want them to learn to work. Jesus wants us to do our work carefully and well. He wants us to learn to be responsible.

If you think the children in the stories are being responsible and doing a good job, put your finger on the Happy Face. If you think the boy or girl is being careless or not doing his or her job well, put your finger on the Stop sign.

"We have a lot of work to do today," announced Daddy. "But if we divide it up and everyone helps, we can leave sooner for the beach."

Rickie waited impatiently for Daddy to give the big boys their chores. "OK, Rickie," Daddy finally said with a smile, "I want you to sweep the kitchen. I know you'll do a good job."

Rickie found the broom and dustpan in the garage. He carefully swept all around the edges of the kitchen. He moved the wastebasket and swept behind it. He swept under the table and around the legs. He had a fine pile of dirt and dust to sweep into the dustpan. Rickie felt proud of the job he had done.

Do you think Rickie was responsible and did his job well? Put your finger on the Happy Face or on the Stop sign to show your answer.

Mitzi watched Mama and wiggled impatiently. Mama frowned at Mitzi and gave her head a quick shake. Mitzi sighed. She knew what the frown and the shaking head meant. Mama was on the phone, and she did not want to be disturbed.

Mitzi wandered into the kitchen with dragging feet. She wished Mama would hurry and hang up the phone so she could get permission to go outside and play. Mitzi pressed her nose against the window in the back door. She could hear Mama talking and talking.

Mitzi sighed and looked around. The dishwasher door was hanging open. Mama had been unloading it when the phone rang. Suddenly Mitzi smiled. She would be helpful while she was waiting! Mitzi began taking the clean dishes out of the dishwasher and putting them away in the cupboard.

Do you think Mitzi has learned to be a good helper? Put your finger on the Happy Face or on the Stop sign to show your answer.

"Jackie," Mama said from the doorway, "please clean up your room now. Remember, Grandma's coming in just two days."

Jackie frowned. She was sitting on the floor in front of two rows of dolls and stuffed animals. She was playing school. There were piles of papers and colored pencils and books beside her on the floor.

"Put your toys and books away in the places they belong," Mama added as she turned to go.

Jackie sat, thinking. She was glad Grandma was coming soon. But she did not want to clean up her room. She might want to play school again tomorrow.

Suddenly Jackie had an idea. If Mama couldn't see her dolls and stuffed animals, she would think they were put away! Jackie carefully covered up all of her playthings with a big, pink blanket.

Do you think Jackie was responsible and cleaned her room well? Put your finger on the Happy Face or on the Stop sign to show your answer.

"Come here, please," Mama called from the kitchen.

Kevin galloped on his broom to the kitchen door. "Stop!" he said to his broom horse.

Mama laughed. "Park your horse for a minute," she said. "I need some help."

Mama gave Kevin a big brown paper bag. "Please go to each bedroom and the bathroom and find all the wastebaskets," she said. "Empty the trash from each wastebasket into this bag."

"OK," said Kevin. The big bag bumped against his legs as he ran to his bedroom.

Kevin held his wastebasket upside down over the bag. Some of the trash fell into the bag. Some Kleenexes fluttered to the floor beside it. Kevin kicked at the Kleenexes on the floor, and then he grabbed the edge of the bag and towed it behind him toward the bathroom.

Do you think Kevin was responsible and did his job well? Put your finger on the Happy Face or on the Stop sign to show your answer.

It is important to learn to be a helper around the house. And it is important to do your jobs well.

What do you do around the house to help your family?

Chapter 9

I Can Choose to Make Good Decisions

These children each have something to decide about how they will act. After each story, I want you to tell me if the decision the boy or girl made was a good one. If it was a good decision, put your finger on the Happy Face. If it was a bad decision, put your finger on the Stop sign.

Sammy stuck his fingers into his ears. But he could still hear Baby Caleb crying. He walked over to the couch where Mama was sitting, trying to get the baby to nurse. "What's wrong with Baby Caleb, Mama?" asked Sammy.

Mama gave Sammy a tired smile. "I think Baby Caleb is cutting some new teeth," she said. "He's a little fussy."

"I want you to play with me, Mama," Sammy said. He held out a finger, and Baby Caleb grabbed it tightly.

"I would like to play with you, Sammy," said Mama, "but I'm very busy right now. If you go to your room and play quietly for a while, I will play with you when Baby Caleb goes to sleep."

"But I want you to play with me *now*!" shouted Sammy. "I want you to play with me *now*!"

Did Sammy make a good decision when he shouted at his mama? Put your finger on the Happy Face or on the Stop sign to show your answer.

30

"It's time for bed, Trevor," said Mama. She closed the worship book she had been reading. "Put the book back on your shelf and go brush your teeth."

"But I'm not tired!" exclaimed Trevor. He bounced off Mama's lap and began to jump around the living room.

"Trevor," said Mama. "Do you remember what we talked about this afternoon? You promised me you would go to bed quietly and happily."

"Oh," said Trevor. "I forgot."

"Well, now I have reminded you," said Mama. "Are you going to be good?"

"Yes!" said Trevor. He stood up straight and tall. "I am going to be *very* good." Trevor went to the bathroom to find his toothbrush.

Did Trevor make a good decision when he decided to go to bed quickly as his mother had asked? Put your finger on the Happy Face or on the Stop sign to show your answer.

"It's time to come inside, Lindsey," called Mama through the kitchen window.

Lindsey kept on swinging.

"Lindsey!" called Mama in a louder voice.

"Please come inside!"

Lindsey kept on swinging.

Mama went to the back door and looked out. "Did you hear me calling you?" she asked.

"I don't want to come in," said Lindsey.

"I'm sorry," said Mama, "but it's time to come in the house."

"I don't want to come in! I want to swing!" shrieked Lindsey. She burst into angry tears.

Did Lindsey make a good decision when she decided to keep swinging and not mind her mama? Put your finger on the Happy Face or on the Stop sign to show your answer.

Remember: You have lots of decisions to make every day about how you are going to act. You have lots of chances to make good decisions. Pray that Jesus will help you to make good decisions.

Closing Note

I hope you have enjoyed the stories in this book. I hope they have helped you think about making good decisions. I hope you will practice making good decisions every day. Jesus will help you make good decisions. Ask Him to help you.

Your family will be proud of you. Jesus will be proud of you. And you will be a happy child.